Disney·PIXAR
THE INCREDIBLES

THE ADVENTURES OF
VIOLET & DASH

Super Sleuths

By
Suzanne Francis

Illustrated by
Melissa Ford and Shiho Tilley

Random House 🏠 New York

J
ADVENTURES OF
VIOLET & DASH

Published in the United States by Random House Children's Books, a division of
Penguin Random House LLC, 1745 Broadway, New York, NY 10019, and in Canada by
Penguin Random House Canada Limited, Toronto, in conjunction with Disney Enterprises, Inc.
Random House and the colophon are registered trademarks of Penguin Random House LLC.

rhcbooks.com

ISBN 978-0-7364-3942-8 (trade) — ISBN 978-0-7364-3943-5 (lib. bdg.)

Printed in the United States of America

10 9 8 7 6 5 4 3 2 1

CHAPTER 1
VIOLET

Hi, Diary.
I'm back.

But are you a "diary," really? I feel like you're more of a brother-sister-bonding therapy session or something. That just sounds sad and weird. We're supposed to be using these pages to solve a mystery, so maybe it's an investigative journal. A <u>Super</u> investigative journal. Eh, what's in a name anyway. It doesn't matter.

So when we last wrote, Dash had a new best friend, Chance, who has shape-shifting Super powers and is a prankster like him. They goofed around and had a lot of fun, but Chance almost got into BIG trouble because of some creepy notes someone was leaving in his locker.

The anonymous notes were from a weirdo asking him to steal school records. Chance was going to do it because he believed it would be good for all Supers. He even tried to get Dash to help. Luckily, Dash wanted nothing to do with it, and Chance ended up realizing the whole thing was a mistake.

So now we're trying to figure out the identity of the creep who left those notes. I'll let Dash fill you in on the details. He and Chance are the lead detectives on this case—but I will tell you that we haven't figured it out yet. Chance hasn't received any more notes, so part of me wonders if we should let it go. I mean, maybe it was just some stupid kid pulling a prank on Dash and Chance. You know, someone getting back at them—giving them a dose of their own medicine.

It's more serious than that, Vi. Doesn't your gut tell you that? Or have you drifted so far into Normalville that you lost your sense of good and evil? Remember? The notes said they KNEW Chance was a Super and it was time to "dominate." That's no innocent prank!

I've been pretty busy at school, so I haven't had too much time to talk to Dash about it. I got stuck working on a massively boring presentation on the anatomy of plant cells with this kid in my class who does more grunting than talking. Gigi (my best friend) and I had planned to pair up, and then the teacher pulled the old "assigned partners" thing. I hate it when he does that. Sometimes I wonder if he can read my mind—how did he know to pair me up with the last person I would EVER choose? Maybe my science teacher is actually a super villain. . . . Now I'm starting to sound like Dash.

YES. I like the way you're thinking, Vi!
If you need someone to investigate,
you know where to find me.

So I created the model for our presentation AND I had to do the bulk of the presenting because my so-called partner left me stranded up there. (Can't say that was much of a surprise.)

I'm not sure if you know this about me yet, but I'm not a big fan of making presentations. Public speaking is definitely NOT one of my Super powers. I'd take fighting a villain over speaking in front of a large group any day of the week. Unfortunately, that wasn't an option here. Thankfully, it's over. And I survived. Barely.

Dash and Chance have been busy working on their powers. All. The. Time. If you ask me, I think they're a little obsessed. Mom and Dad don't want us using our powers unless we really have to (they had no complaints when we helped rescue them from the Screenslaver, of course). For the most part, as far as daily life goes . . . they want us to just act like normal kids.

But we're NOT NORMAL KIDS!
We're AWESOME HEROES!

I know they wouldn't be happy if they found out how much Dash has been practicing, but I'm not going to rat him out. He's been sparring with

Chance down in the basement at every opportunity. And since Dash is a trouble magnet, I'm thinking it may not be a bad thing for him to be safe at home with Chance.

You'll thank me the next time a super villain comes around—I will be MORE than ready for anything they throw at us.

I've been taking a little break from using my powers. I can't even remember the last time I used them. Oh, wait. Okay, so I did put Dash in a force field last night when he spilled popcorn all over my room and then tried to bolt before cleaning it up.

But other than that . . . Oh, wait. I also had to throw one around my cell model for science yesterday, when Jack-Jack was doing his laser-beam eye thingy. (There was NO WAY I was going to let him destroy my project—it took too long to make!)

I think that's just one of life's necessities when you have a baby brother with random powers that strike at any moment. Now that I think about it, I probably use my powers against the evil forces of brothers more than anything else! *awesome*

I've been hanging out with Gigi a lot, too—but I can't use my powers in front of her. For all she knows, I'm completely normal. And that's the way I have to keep it. Normal has been fun, though.

normal = boring

I mean, sure, it is a little weird not being able to tell my best friend that I'm able to vanish into thin air or create nearly indestructible force fields, but . . .

well, it is what it is. I guess it's also extra weird because her uncle is Frozone. It'd be awesome if she knew about him.

I actually have no idea if she's aware of her uncle's powers. If she knew about him, then maybe I could tell her about my powers. Every now and then, she makes a comment when his name comes up that makes me wonder if she knows. Like the other day, when she told me she couldn't go to the movies, she said, "Uncle Lucius is coming by to take me and my little sister out for frozen yogurt." And when she said "frozen," she kind of looked at me in a weird way. I wanted to ask her SOOO bad. But I didn't. If she doesn't know about his secret life as a Super, I'd mess everything up for him. And I definitely do not want to (and CANNOT) do that. We all know—

our identity is our most valuable possession

(as Mom likes to tell us ten million times a day), so I definitely have to keep my mouth shut.

At the moment, the best thing to do is just focus on my normal side and enjoy doing normal stuff with my normal best friend—

and
I'm
cool
with
that.

Speaking
of normal . . .

I have some news.

The rec center is starting up this new after-school program.

I guess they're going to have different activities—sports, arts and crafts, games, stuff like that.

My parents signed Dash and me up! They keep telling us we need to be

"well-rounded,"

and of course, they're all about getting us involved in normal activities. Typically, I wouldn't be too thrilled about it, but Gigi's parents signed her up, too, so I know it will be fun. We're going to do

together. I'm kind of excited because it'll be great to get some extra time with her every day.

CHAPTER 2
DASH

Hello, Ace. Yeah, it's been a little while. We've all been busy. But before I get to the latest and greatest on the mystery of the EVIL NOTE WRITER, I gotta say this to my sis: Why, why, WHY do you have to put down my desire to be the SUPEREST SUPER I can be? It seems like you want to pretend you don't even have powers. Are you CRAZY?! Powers aren't just for making awesome brothers angry or defending your stuff against crazy laser-monster babies. If you ask me, you need to embrace who you are and be your best! Practice makes perfect, right? What if you worked on your force-field powers and started to create even

BIGGER force fields? Maybe you could put a
whole house in a force field . . . or a

whole city . . .

or maybe even the

WHOLE PLANET!

That would be
wicked awesome!!!!

And don't you think it's kind of phony, acting like you don't even have powers? Ever? I get that Mom and Dad want us to act normal, but I don't see what's wrong with practicing in secret. As long as nobody sees us, what's the problem? Then when we DO need to use our powers (like against Syndrome, the Underminer, and the Screenslaver), we will be ready.

SHARK ATTACK!

Normal Vi not using her powers

So, my personal opinion: don't forget about your powers. You know how we go the whole summer without playing the stupid recorder, and then when we go back to music class, Ms. Dermilio says,

"You're a disgrace to music!"

And we're like,

"What do I do with this strange piece of plastic again?"

Without practice, we forget. I'm not saying I want to practice the recorder over the summer—it's a (metfur.) My English teacher is all about them lately, so I guess they're in my brain.

It's called a metaphor, genius.

With powers as cool as yours, you should practice to be your best. Yeah, I know you didn't ask, but I'm telling you anyway. The Dash's two cents. And each Dash cent has gotta be worth at least five hundred bucks.

Also, you seem to forget one of the main reasons why we've been working so hard:

Chance.

His parents don't even know he has powers.

You and I are the ONLY ones who know. . . .

Well, us and that weirdo who wrote those notes, I guess.
More on that in a minute.

And Chance is still learning about his abilities—do you remember when you first discovered you had powers? I bet you can't even remember that day. We're a step ahead of him because we've had people with powers around us our whole lives. Chance is just learning about all this stuff—he doesn't have the knowledge we have. And our practice sessions? They're really working—Chance is getting better with his transformations. And I know I'm not a therapist or anything

(though I think I probably could be, because I am clearly a DEEP WELL of wisdom),

but it seems like Chance is getting more confident.

You and I both know how much confidence helps when it comes to using your powers. Remember when you thought you couldn't create a force field on that island and you almost got us killed? Then you were like,

"I can do it!"
and
BAM!

you saved us.

Without confidence, we could have been killed. I mean, if we don't have that, we might as well not be Supers. Anyway, we've been practicing, and the other day, Chance was able to transform into a cobra and a clone of me all on his own. He says once he knows an animal or a person well enough, he can shift without needing to look at a picture. (I still can't get used to seeing a clone of myself in front of me—

that'll ALWAYS be weird.)

Now we're working to see if we can expand his list of transformations. He shifted for almost a whole minute! His record before that was only 35 seconds! There's nothing wrong with trying to be your Superest, sis. Nothing at all. You should give it a try.

Of course, our training is now going to hit a major snag because of those dumb classes at the rec center you're all excited about. Why Mom and Dad had to do that to us is beyond me. You can be all "I can't wait!" about it, but I know better. It's going to be a colossal waste of time. What are we going to do? Make friendship bracelets, weave pot holders, and sing around a campfire?

"Sing around a campfire"? It's an after-school program, not summer camp.

Either that or it's going to be like an extension of school—and who wants a LONGER school day?

Not me.

But I'm stuck going, and there's nothing I can do about it. Well . . . we'll see. Maybe I can run around the rec center for three hours and no one will miss me. That would give me time to think about our perp. We haven't pegged the guy who left those notes in Chance's locker yet. And, Vi, anybody who tries to convince someone to steal school records is NOT a prankster. Come on.

I think all that normal stuff is making your brain mushy. That's

wayyyyy

more villain than prankster. And one thing we learned from that drama is that we need to be on alert at all times.

We ARE going to catch this perp—our thorough investigation is already under way.

First,
let's review
our clues.

We know the perp wanted to steal school records and told Chance that they were going to use them to expose a super villain at school.

And thankfully, we still have the notes Chance saved.

EVIDENCE #1

I know who you are, Chance. And I know your secret. I have a mission that only you can accomplish. If you accept, respond to this note and put it back in your locker.

EVIDENCE #2

You are a Super. There's no shame in it. I'm a Super, too. If you're tired of hiding your true self, join me. I have a plan that will help Supers everywhere. It's our time to dominate!

My take: NO ONE is innocent without proof. Even Vi, Chance, and I were on the first list of suspects when we started. We're leaving NO PERSON unturned! Here's our latest list (Chance and I had like 153 people on the original list, but we've done a lot of work to cut it down).

1. Gigi (Vi's best friend). Likelihood rating: 25%. Okay, fine. She's probably NOT a villain. But her friendship with Vi was strangely timed with the appearance of the notes, so that made us seriously consider her innocence. . . .

You guys are insane. Gigi is NOT a villain! JEEEEZ!

2. A rabid squirrel from outer space. LR: 0% ~~5%~~. This seemed possible, but we eliminated it the other day after really talking it out.

3. Lunch Lady Margie. LR: 4%. She weighs about 350 pounds, has hands the size of baseball mitts, and slings burgers onto plates like a pro wrestler knocking out a fly. We think she's hiding something. But the likelihood of that being a secret desire to snag school records (either to smoke out a super villain or do whatever) . . . not so sure. I think the only thing she's TRULY hiding is the fact that she coughs over the food.

4. Ecnahc and Hsad. LR: 10%. If there are exact opposite versions of Chance and me in another dimension and they manage to come into our dimension and wreak havoc, they'd be evil and weird because we're so amazingly awesome.

5. Mom and Dad. LR: 10%. I wrote this one off quickly, but then I started thinking—what if they're doing this as some kind of freaky TEST? Like, to see what I do. This is the kind of thinking I'm talking about. You have to dig deep! Right? Then I started flipping out, trying to figure out what they would want me to do, and I figured if it was a test, I totally passed. But then—why would they test Chance?

UNLESS they are that sneaky. But this conversation can go on for a really long time, so I'm thinking we should just leave it at 10% and move on. But would they . . . ?

Seriously? Hate to tell you, but Mom and Dad have way better things to do than write creepy notes to your friend to "test" you.

6. Jason. LR: 70%. This guy is our top suspect, and I'm beginning to think he should move up to 80%. Maybe even 83% (our mathematical system is very specific). He's a sixth grader who had to move his locker earlier in the year because it was busted or something—and now it's near Chance's. And guess what? That was right before the whole mess started. Coincidence? You decide. Plus, he seemed normal when he first showed up (normal for a sixth grader), but then all of a sudden, he started being kind of rude—giving us funny looks and stuff. I realized that all this started happening RIGHT AFTER Chance and I battled it out over the school records. It makes sense—he's mad that Chance didn't follow through and I stopped him, so now he's taking it out on us. But I see you, Jason. I see you.

Guess what, Ace?! Great news. Chance convinced his parents to sign him up for the boring rec-center program! Now we can both be tortured ... and continue to work on cracking this case—together.

CHAPTER 3
VIOLET
AND
DASH

Those are all very . . . interesting theories, Dash, but I don't think Jason is your perp. He might be a little odd, but he doesn't seem like a bad kid to me. What do you mean, he's rude? It sounds like a stretch—like you're really desperate for a suspect. And I get it. I'd like to know who wrote those notes, too. But maybe we should give it a rest for a while. Chance hasn't heard from the mystery note writer again, and—I don't know. Don't you think it would be good to focus on something else? Like the rec center! Gigi and I took a jewelry-making class and it was super cool. We even signed up for a booth at the craft fair. Gigi thinks we can make some serious money. Check out some of our designs!

These are my favorites:

Seriously. Give yourselves a little break from the detective work and just try having some normal kid fun for a change. You need to find a balance. I get that you think you know it all, but I am older and wiser, so you should listen to me for once.

Violet, Violet, Violet. We are NOT backing down on our detective work. Not. Backing. Down. That's what the perp WANTS. And we are not in the business of giving perps what they want. We are in the business of bringing them to justice! We added a suspect today. Likelihood rating is a whopping 75%. You ready? THE SCREENSLAVER.

Picture this: Evelyn what's-her-face manages to manipulate some kid

(perhaps, oh . . . I don't know . . . JASON?)

with a pair of those wacky hypno-goggles.

Now she controls what he does. Right? So—she makes the perp put the notes in Chance's locker so SHE can have some Supers bust her out of jail. Okay, maybe it's a 60% LR.

On the upside, I will say that the after-school boringness was better than expected. Okay, it wasn't boring at all. Except for the craft activity they made us do. Weaving pot holders. Not even kidding! Chance and I laughed our butts off when the counselor—who was your weird friend Kari—started handing out looms.

Don't be mean.
Kari is nice! At least you
know she'll be enthusiastic
about everything.

She said we're supposed to weave as many
pot holders as we can, and they're going to
sell them at that lame-o craft fair to help
pay for more pot-holder materials so more
kids can make more pot holders to sell, and
so on and so on. What's the point? How about
we skip the looming and go play basketball
instead?

The best thing about the rec center was this sports class we got to take. Our counselor's name is Victor, and he was probably the coolest guy I've ever met—like, even cooler than Jim, that guy with the hair and sunglasses from swim school. Anyway, I think Victor goes to your school. Do you know him?

Yes—he's a new kid. I think he's in one of Gigi's classes.

He said we can decide what we want to do each day, as long as we're moving our bodies and not sitting around like slugs— which is pretty awesome. He said he's not into being still and lazy. Sounds like the perfect counselor for me, right? Today we played basketball, and tomorrow we're going to hike up to some crazy rock formation— I didn't even know we had rock formations here. Mom and Dad could totally tell that I had fun, and they acted all know-it-all-y about it. Like, without saying anything.

"So, how was it?" asked Mom in her "I-know-the-answer" tone.

But it's okay. I can admit I was wrong. Okay? And I'm sooo glad I was wrong.

Something else happened today. Jason is suspectio numero uno. (Yeah, pretty sure

I scored a solid A on my Spanish test.)

Here's what happened: Chance and I got stuck after class with Mr. Kropp because we were talking during another one of his boring lectures. Then we missed the bus to the rec center. Which actually ended up being a good thing, because while we were outside, we overheard Jason talking to some of his friends. (Vi, if I had your powers, I would have totally disappeared and walked right up to them, but anyway.) This is what we heard:

JASON: Supers mumble mumble. Lame. Elastigirl mumble mumble. Weak.

ME (whispering): SHHH! Listen.

(Chance nodded and we both stopped talking.)

JASON: All those guys—Frozone . . . the whole crew of them. They're all so dumb and weak. I'd want to meet a villain over one of those lame Supers any day. Villains are wayyy more interesting. I mean, come on. Mr. Incredible? An old guy with muscles?

Please.

Chance and I looked at each other and bolted. So yeah, Jason just zoomed to the top of the list.

JASON = GUILTY!

See, Violet?

GUILTY!

He said WHAT about Dad?!? Saying those things about Supers doesn't necessarily make Jason guilty of writing those notes, but it does make him really dumb (and just plain wrong)!

We need a trap to catch Jason in the act. And I actually have the perfect plan: we'll bait him with a note from Chance, and then we'll be there when he writes back. Maybe

those pot holders will come
in handy. . . . Some other
possible traps . . .
Hmmm . . .

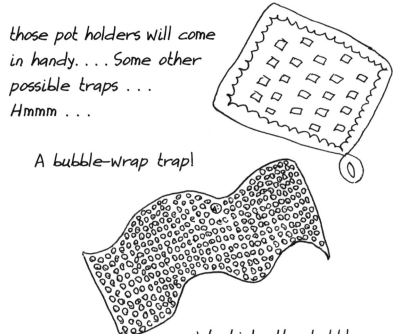

A bubble-wrap trap!

We hide the bubble
wrap under a rug, and when Jason steps on
it, the bubbles burst, scaring the heck out
of him. He falls to the ground, causing more
bubbles to pop, and we drop the pot-holder
trap on him!

Or maybe we dig a big,
deep hole and fill it with glue.
We cover it with something so
he doesn't see it, and when
he falls in, he'll be stuck!

Glue

Why not just fill the pit with killer sharks?

YESSS!

That's what I'm talking about!

After I slept on it, I changed my mind. As awesome as all those ideas are, they sound like a lot of work. We wanted to keep it simple.

Here's the new plan:

Once Jason is near Chance's locker, Chance and I will get into a big blowout fight.

Fake,
of course.

The whole thing will be scripted, so we'll get to use our sweet acting skills—I'm pretty sure we're both extremely convincing in a

"natural talent"
sort of way.

CHANCE: What's wrong with you, Dash?
Why would you do that?!

DASH: Um, I think you know why I did
it, Chance.

CHANCE: I can't believe we're still
talking about this. You're such
a BABY, Dash.

DASH: Oh, that again? You know what?
I'm not stooping to your level.
I'm outta here.

It's going to be all dramatic, and we're
going to make sure we do it when Jason
is around. He'll think Chance and I aren't

friends anymore. Chance used to communicate with the perp by leaving notes in his own locker, so after our argument, Chance is going to leave the note sort of sticking out of his locker as a lure.

Soon Jason will be putty in our hands!

That's when we'll pounce!

I have to say, I think this is a pretty terrible idea. Can't you just try being normal . . . like, for one single day???

CHAPTER 4
DASH

Today was crazy.

Remember our plan?

Well, we tried it—sort of. We wrote that note I was telling you about, the one we were going to leave in Chance's locker. Chance was on the fence about it, but I kinda convinced him to do it. Well, at least I THOUGHT I did. Here's what we wrote. We changed it a bunch of times until we got it just right. And of course, I made sure Chance wrote it since Jason would recognize his handwriting. It's not amateur hour here!

Hey, man, I've been thinking about it. I made a mistake. I'm ready to <u>dominate</u>. Can you give me another chance? I have a plan. Let me know when we can meet.

The "another chance" idea was mine. Pretty good, right?!

Sometimes I even impress myself.

Yup. You're a real genius, Dash.

Then we got into the big dramatic fight in front of Jason. When Jason got to his locker, I stomped up to Chance and we started our act. Right on cue, Jason stood and gawked—we were really convincing. I could feel it! We were in the moment!

Then I walked off in a huff. Chance took our note from his bag and left it sticking out of his locker. The plan worked like a well-oiled machine up to that point.

Chance and I planned to meet up again at the rec center. As always, I got there first. When Chance arrived, I asked him how the plan went and he was acting all weird and quiet. Finally, he confessed. . . .

HE DIDN'T LEAVE THE NOTE!!!

I asked him what happened, and he got all mad, saying stuff like I was pressuring him to do it and he didn't feel ready . . . and he started asking me if I remembered what got him into trouble in the first place. Then he ran off! "Didn't feel ready"? And yeah—of course I remember what started all the trouble. If he'd stuck around, I would have reminded him we were already IN trouble with this creep. I mean, what did Chance want to do?

Hide? Give up? Not me!
I'm THE DASH!

I followed Chance out behind the rec center and saw him running away. I used my super speed to catch up to him easily enough, but it was obvious that he wanted to get away from me. What the heck?!

And come on. Did he really think running away from me was even possible? Without warning, he shape-shifted into a falcon and managed to escape for about a millisecond. I kept on him until his clock ran out and he turned back into himself. I'd say it was probably very close to his 60-second record. He was all out of breath.

CHANCE: I looked up the fastest animal in the world . . . and I still couldn't get away from you.

ME: Falcon?

(He nodded, too out of breath to even speak. That makes ME the fastest animal in the world!)

second fastest in the world

ME: That's a new one. You transformed without looking at a card?

CHANCE: Yeah, I studied it for a while. Watched some videos and stuff.

ME: Nice. (Then I remembered how annoyed I was at him.) But what the heck, Chance?? Why didn't you leave the note, like we planned?

CHANCE: I knew you'd be mad. Sorry, but I just couldn't do it. I felt like it would get us into trouble again. I guess I chickened out.

I felt kind of bad for him when he admitted he was scared. I know Chance has confidence issues, but it's not like I was going to dump him as a friend just because he ruined my amazingly genius plan. I also realized that maybe, just maybe, I was being a little bit pushy. You know, carried away by the awesomeness of my plan?

No. You? Pushy? I can't believe that.

So I apologized to Chance. We were about to head back to the rec center—we figured Kari the pot-holder queen still had our looms ready and waiting. But then we heard some weird noises coming from the woods. It sounded like someone yelling. Being the detectives we are, we followed the sounds to investigate.

We saw this big old abandoned-looking building and saw a window way up high—too high to reach. Chance turned back into a falcon and flew up to one of the windows. I wasn't gonna miss out, so I backed up, ran right up the wall as fast as I could, and landed on the window ledge. We both peeked in. It was an old gym with dusty floor mats and stuff all over—and you'll never guess what we saw. . . .

Victor, our counselor from the sports class, was floating in the air. That's right,
FLOATING!
His entire body was lifted up over these weird foam spikes.

He floated up a bit and then fell, hitting the spikes. He was obviously frustrated. Chance and I watched as he tried again and again. Floating, then falling, then starting over again. We were in complete shock. We could not believe Victor had

SUPER POWERS! WHAAAAT??????

Chance's transformation time had run out—we were both so focused on Victor that neither of us was keeping track. So he turned back into himself without being prepared and grabbed on to me. Before we knew it, we had tumbled through the open window! Luckily, we landed in a big pit of foam pieces. Victor was shocked to see us. As we tried to climb out of the foam pit, he walked over, all embarrassed. He was like,

"Oh, hey, guys. Didn't see you there. I was just trying out this magic trick. My uncle's a magician."

Chance and I knew he was lying! He started talking about how he was studying to be a magician, and it was his lifelong dream.

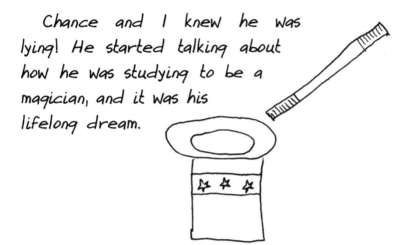

I couldn't let him continue. Finally, I said,

"Can we see that again?"

Victor got all shy and was like,

"No, no, I'm out of practice. When I get it right, I can show it to you."

And stuff like that. Then he started to move toward the door, trying to end the conversation.

Chance and I looked at each other. What could we do? We knew we were supposed to protect our identity, but with another Super . . . especially one who seemed so . . . alone and embarrassed? It didn't feel right not to tell him we were just like him. We huddled up and quickly talked it out while Victor stood there, squirming like a worm on a hook. Chance felt extra bad for him because he knew how it felt to be clueless and alone with your powers. We knew we had to share our secret with Victor. Do you have any idea how cool it is to meet another Super kid??

Ummm, NO. Wish I did!

After we made our decision, we walked over to Victor. He looked really nervous and uncomfortable.

ME: Don't worry. We're just like you.

VICTOR: You like magic, too?

CHANCE: *No, we're Supers . . . just like you.*

Then, to prove his point, Chance transformed into a clone of Victor. Victor shouted in surprise and fell over one of the foam spikes. After a second, he burst out laughing. He was so happy and relieved. He told us that he didn't know anyone else with powers, and nobody knew about his.

"Well, nobody except you guys, now . . . ," he said.

"Wow, we're pretty similar," Chance replied.

"I didn't know any Supers either before Dash. I barely even knew how to use my powers!"

We talked for a while, and he explained that he was practicing in the old gym. He wants to hone his levitation powers, make them better. He showed us the rest of the gym and everything he has set up. There's this crazy obstacle course for testing and training Super powers!

It was amazing!

Victor asked us what we were doing out in the woods, and we told him a little bit about Jason and how we wondered if Jason was a Super, too. We didn't go into the whole thing, but we told him we were suspicious. Victor nodded like he completely understood and said,

"Sit tight for the next few days and let me check him out for you guys."

He said he'd be happy to help us—especially since he appreciated having us as his first Super friends.

We even got to try out some of the obstacles:

climbing ropes,
zip-lining,
climbing walls

(in my case, running up them).

It was AWESOME. Climbing the ropes was really cool because it got me thinking—if I work my arms and hands so they can catch up to the speed of my feet, then maybe I can

CLIMB SUPER FAST, TOO!

Then Chance really showed off his shape-shifting skills to our new friend. I had a running list in my mind of all the animals he could transform into without looking at his cards. So I called out each one and he shifted on cue. It was easiest for him to shift into animals that he actually knew. He had been feeding his neighbor's cat while she was away, so he was at the top of his game with that one.

Cat—easy!

Dog—yup!

Lizard—piece of cake!

I kept it fun and didn't push his time with any of them. Figured we didn't need to throw that into the mix while he was showing off to Victor.

Chance did a great job!

Then we headed back to the rec center and played basketball with our group. It was cool, but nothing could compare to that gym! Victor told us we could visit as often as we like—as long as we keep it a secret. So now we're super-secret gym members.

How awesome is that?

Vi, you need to come check it out. I can't wait to go back!

I can't believe you found another Super. What are you—a Super magnet? Why don't I ever meet any Supers?!? I just hope Victor is trustworthy. It sounds like you told him a lot about yourselves. The gym sounds interesting, but is it safe? I will definitely come by and check it out.

CHAPTER 5
VIOLET

I checked out the secret gym for myself. I went with Dash and Chance to meet Victor and make sure this was all okay. I had to make up a story and skip some jewelry time with Gigi, which made me feel kind of bad, but how could I tell her where I was really going? Plus, it's my sisterly duty to keep tabs on Dash, and I had to see what he was getting into with this.

And yes, my parents' rule about keeping our identities secret was on my mind all day long. But when I actually got to the gym and met Victor (who does seem cool, by the way), I felt like the rule didn't apply. It was great to meet a new Super and have this kind of . . . instant connection. Something I had never experienced before. So I just went with it. Victor convinced me to try some of the obstacles. There were ropes, balance beams, and barriers to go through as Victor used a machine to shoot tennis balls at me! It was fun trying to finish the course while defending myself against evil tennis balls!

You were awesome!

The four of us had a great time with the course and setting up little challenges for each other. I worked on trying to stretch the limits of my force field by trying to include more and more stuff from the gym. Dash zipped around and pushed stuff into different configurations while I tried to see how big I could make the force fields. We also worked on some combination moves. In one, Dash pushed me really fast on a scooter so I could quickly throw force fields at various targets.

When we took a break, Victor said he had checked out Jason. He'd

"had a little chat with him,"

but he didn't go into specifics about their conversation. Victor's not sure whether Jason's guilty . . .

but he definitely thinks Jason's a Normal,

as he calls people without Super powers. We were talking about whether we think the mystery writer is a Super, and Victor says he's 99% sure that the answer is no. Victor believes Supers are good. Of course, Dash brought up an obvious point: super villains. He was like,

"They have Super powers and they're not good. What if the perp is a super villain?"

We talked about it for a long time, and Victor seemed completely convinced that whoever wrote the note was not a Super.

Victor told us he didn't think we should worry about Jason.

"He's not worth your time,"

he said.

Dash and Chance seemed disappointed that Jason wasn't the perp, but I wouldn't put it past them to keep investigating. . . .

On the upside, we all agreed that the gym is a super-cool place. Dash and Chance feel like they're really working toward their full potential, and I can't say I disagree. And maybe they're right—maybe we should be ready for anything.

We are definitely right. I'm keeping my eyes open. Always scanning for trouble at lightning speed.

CHAPTER 6
DASH

I know Victor said not to worry about Jason, but guess what?

He was wrong!

If we had any doubt before (and THE DASH, for one, DID NOT), Jason's LR has moved up to 95% now. He bumped into Chance on the way out of school today! No apology. No nothing. It was completely on purpose! I know what you're thinking, Vi, but I can guarantee—it was ON PURPOSE! We could feel it. Chance even fell to the ground, and what did Jason do? Hopped on his bike and took off. NOT the actions of an innocent guy.

Sorry, but I can't help it! Are you sure it wasn't an accident? It's pretty crowded after the bell, so it's possible that Jason didn't know he knocked into Chance that hard.

I wanted to sprint after Jason soooo bad. Let's face it—I could have used my Super speed to knock him off his bike without him even SEEING me. But I knew that wouldn't solve anything. We gotta catch him in the act, and to do that, we have to be smart. And I know how to be smart.

Chance dusted himself off and I asked him if he was okay. He nodded and said,

"Yup. Thanks."

I knew he was embarrassed, so I tried to make him laugh. I said,

"At least it wasn't in front of the whole school or anything."

Yeah, it was a dumb joke, I'll admit. They can't all be gems.

He kind of forced a smile and said,

"Right."

After that, we really didn't say much to each other. It was kind of weird—

you know those moments when it's quiet and you don't know what to say,

so it feels weird that it's quiet? And then it just starts to feel

weirder
and
weirder

because the more you think about it, the weirder it seems, and then you start thinking that the other person thinks it's weird, and that only makes it weirder because you start wondering what they're thinking about and why they're not saying anything and then you remember you have nothing to say and it's like this

cycle of quiet
Weirdness
where every minute
feels like twenty?

⊰ ✿ · ✿ · ✿·✿ · ✿ · ✿·✿ · ✿ · ✿·✿ ⊱

Yes. It's called an awkward silence. And I know it well.

⊰ ✿ · ✿ · ✿·✿ · ✿ · ✿·✿ · ✿ · ✿·✿ ⊱

Anyway, we got to the gym and I tried
to get Chance to forget about Jason, but I
could tell he was distracted.

Can't say
I blame him.

Victor asked us what was going on, and Chance told him the story. Victor got mad and started talking about how Jason shouldn't treat people that way. He said if Jason knew Chance was a Super, he would never have the guts to treat him like that. He was saying things like

"If he knew you had powers, he'd be kissing the ground you walk on."

He was starting to sound a little crazy, and we started to regret saying anything.

That's . . . intense.

At that point, Chance started to wonder whether it was just an accident. I wasn't sure if he was trying to downplay it or if he actually believed it. But that didn't matter to Victor.

He said Jason should have apologized.

I don't know why Victor is so sure that Jason isn't a Super. Like I said, I think Jason should be at the top of our suspects list. It was great that Victor wanted to help us figure out the identity of the perp, but it's up to us to figure out what to do next. We can't have someone else swooping in to solve this problem for us.

We're Supers.
We don't need to be rescued.
WE do the rescuing!

But you know what that means? The investigation is officially back open! Time to put on our thinking caps, because we need a plan.

My thinking cap

CHAPTER 7
VIOLET

Bad day, diary-journal-log, whatever you are. Really bad day. So—I couldn't stop thinking about the whole Jason thing, and basically my big-sister-worry brain kicked in. Hard. I think Victor's reaction made me feel like I had to get fired up even more than I normally would—like, it fueled the fire. Anyway, without really knowing exactly what I would do, I tucked my supersuit into my backpack before leaving for school.

I didn't have a plan, but I knew I had to do SOMETHING. It just felt like it was time for me to do a little investigating of my own.

WHOA. Who are you, and what have you done with my sister?

I told Gigi I might be a little late to the rec center (which wasn't a total lie). She seemed a bit annoyed, but I knew I could figure out what to do about that later. Then I got out of my last class a little early, put on my suit, vanished, and headed over to Dash's school, which is my old school. Being invisible makes it easy to get around without getting caught. And I didn't need to deal with the mean old orange-lipstick lady at the security desk. Definitely don't miss her. Anyway, I slipped into the school and started creeping around in search of Jason.

When I finally found him, he was in the gym. They had a special guest teacher showing everyone how to square dance.

YEEEE-HAW!

There's a valuable life skill. I remember doing that back in the day. It was the worst. When am I ever going to use that again? File it with all the math we had to learn just so we could pass a test. Anyway, it was kind of hilarious watching all the awkward kids being forced to do-si-do and stuff, but I couldn't sit around and watch.

SQUARE DANCING?? I hope
I'm sick that day!

I spotted everyone's book bags sitting in a pile in the corner by the bleachers. I scored and found Jason's bag really quickly. It wasn't hard to guess which one was his. I picked out a dirty olive-green bag with stuff like

"Haters Club"
and
"Pig Snot"

scribbled on it.

I slowly slid the bag out, unzipped it, and . . . bingo. Inside were crusty, ripped notebooks with his name on them. I felt kind of creepy going through somebody's things, but I reminded myself that it was for a good cause. This Jason kid was picking on my brother and Chance!

But as I searched his bag, nothing looked suspicious: the notebooks, some crumpled-up homework, a pencil, a pack of gum, some sheet music, and a bunch of crumbs at the bottom. The bag was gross, actually.

I was just about to give up my search when I notice a zippered pocket on the side. I peeked inside and saw

THREE OF CHANCE'S ANIMAL CARDS!

Jason's guilty! TOLD YOU!!!

I was so surprised by the cards that I fell backward and landed on my butt with a thud. All the square-dancing kids stopped what they were doing and looked over at the bags. Even though I was invisible and knew they couldn't see me, I froze. The kids brushed it off as a strange noise and went back to their awkward dance moves. But here's the worst part: The three animal cards I found? They were the T. rex, the rhino, and the eagle. Do I need to explain why this is so freaky? They were the

EXACT SAME

cards Chance used to shape-shift when he and Dash were fighting over the stolen records!

A flash of that weird pins-and-needles feeling rushed through my body as I carefully put the cards back into the zippered pocket. I stumbled again as I got up, which made the entire class look in my direction. The teacher started walking toward the pile of bags, so I booked it.

I ran straight out of the school with thoughts racing through my brain. . . .

How had Jason gotten those cards?

He had to be guilty, right?

But also—I was there the day Dash and Chance were fighting.

Did Jason see me using my powers?

Does he know my identity, too?!?

This is a major disaster.

A VILLAIN WHO KNOWS OUR SECRET IDENTITIES—YEAH! DEFINITELY A MAJOR DISASTER!

When I finally made it to the rec center, I was hoping to find Dash and Chance, but I ran into Gigi instead. She looked at me all confused and was like,

"Hey. I was looking everywhere for you."

I tried to cover by saying,

"Oh, I was looking for you, too."

But she totally knew I was lying. Her face twisted up all weird and she said,

"The jewelry room's in the back of the building. Thought you were going to meet me there."

It just went from bad to worse as I stumbled over my words. I couldn't tell her about anything that was going on, and I was still anxious about the stuff with Jason, so I tried to come up with a lie. I'm definitely not great at making up stories on the spot. I felt horrible about the whole thing. I just sighed and apologized. I didn't know what else to do. Because I couldn't explain, all I could say was

"I'm sorry."

Gigi frowned and said,

"I really could have used your help for the craft fair tomorrow. We signed up to do this together, but you keep disappearing, and you won't tell me where you're going. I know something is going on. Real friends don't hide stuff from each other."

I tried to convince her I wasn't hiding anything by changing the subject. Finally, she just stormed off. I couldn't even follow her—I mean, what would I say?

"Yup, I lied.
And I can't tell you why."

That sounds like a good foundation for a long-lasting friendship—NOT. And besides, I knew I had to find Dash and Chance.

Then I saw Victor.

"Hey, Vi. You okay?"

he asked. I just let out a giant sigh because I wasn't. He asked me if I wanted to head over to the gym with him. I told him that was exactly where I was headed, so we walked over together. He told me about some cool combo thing Chance and Dash were working on and tried to make me laugh. Victor did cheer me up a bit, but it was hard to think straight. Between finding Chance's cards and lying to Gigi,

my head was spinning like a top.

I guess Victor could sense something was wrong, because he started telling me how hard it is to be friends with Normals. It was like he was reading my mind—he said,

"Friends are supposed to be able to share stuff, especially cool stuff, and really . . . what's cooler than Super powers?"

I hate to admit it because I love Gigi, but everything Victor was saying is true—sometimes it feels nearly impossible to truly be friends with someone who doesn't have powers . . .

someone I can't talk to about my Super stuff.

I always thought that having a normal friend or being a Normal would solve everything, but the fact is, I'm a Super and I'll always be one. There's no getting around that.

But Gigi is the coolest friend I've ever had, and I don't want to screw that up. Maybe we can work everything out at the fair tomorrow. I wish none of this had ever happened. I hate the thought of mind-wiping, but right about now, it feels like it would be really handy.

I envy Dash and Chance—at least they can share

EVERYTHING.

Something scary like this happens and you want to be able to talk to your best friend about it.

Right?
It must be nice.

Just tell her! She probably knows about Lucius anyway! She's been a good friend to you—while she's not out planning her Super-Villainous Plots (KIDDING). She'll understand and keep your secret.

I owe Gigi a real apology, but more importantly, what the heck are we going to do about Jason?? I need to think.

I'll tell you what we're going to do . . .
We're going to catch him!
No time to think, Vi. This is serious.

CHAPTER 8
VIOLET AND DASH

Okay. I'm still trying to process everything that just happened. It's like my brain is in overdrive trying to figure it all out. I'm not clear on all the details, but I'll share what I know. First of all—the craft fair. Gigi didn't even show up! I went to our booth early to set up (I definitely owed her for all the preparation she did). I was hoping I could smooth things over with her, but she wasn't there. And Gigi is NEVER late. She's one of those people who is always early—to everything. I knew something was up. I packed all our stuff and went looking for her. I ended up finding her in the last place I expected to see her: the secret gym! From there, things went completely insane. Like. Completely. INSANE.

Here's an entry from Gigi—I asked her to write down EVERYTHING that happened to her:

All right, Vi. I'm writing everything down here for your journal/adventure notebook thingy. I'm going to be completely honest (unlike some people). Anyway, here goes. . . .

First off, I really wasn't sure whether I was going to do the booth at the craft fair with you because I was pretty angry. You'd been acting so weird lately—skipping out on me and making up weird stories. I would've understood if you were busy, but I could tell that you were lying to me. You're my best friend, and I would tell you ANYTHING—so it felt pretty horrible to know you were hiding stuff from me. I was so disappointed.

Anyway. I was sitting by the benches near the playground trying to figure out whether to show up to the booth when Victor walked up to me. I thought he was going to ask me about homework or something, but instead he started talking about you, Vi.

He gave me this whole big speech about how bad you felt that you had argued with me the day before. I was totally taken off guard. Why was Victor talking to me about YOU and ME? I'm thinking, "I had no idea Vi even knew who Victor WAS, but they're good enough friends to be talking about ME?"

He's saying stuff like "Vi was lying to you, but she really wanted to tell you the truth," and "She feels really bad about the whole thing, 'cause you're her best friend, blah, blah, blah." And I'm thinking, "You mean, I WAS her best friend."

THEN he starts taking part of the blame. He goes, "It's partly my fault she couldn't tell you everything. She was kind of protecting me." I had no idea what this guy was talking about.

Then he says, "Vi sent me to get you. Come with me, and everything will make sense."

Of course, I did think it was kind of weird. Part of me was a little afraid. I started to wonder—did something bad happen to you? Victor made it sound like you needed me. I wanted to ignore him and walk away, but I was worried. So I agreed, and he took me to the old gym.

When we got there, Victor told me the door was jammed, so we had to use a ladder to get in. I went first, but when I reached the top of the ladder, Victor pushed me through a small opening at the top of the building. It was completely dark inside, and when I tried to look around, the floor beneath my feet suddenly dropped out from under me! I fell into this weird cage-like thing, and when I looked down, I saw I was hanging directly above a huge tank of water!

It looked something like this:

I had no idea what was going on. Was I in danger? Was this some sort of weird prank? You're always talking about how Dash and Chance are so into pranks. Were they part of this joke? If they were, they would not be laughing by the time I got out of there!

I heard the door slam and called out for Victor, but he didn't answer. I called your name, Vi, but still, nothing. It was quiet and dark. Victor was gone, and I was trapped, all alone.

Okay, so we have Gigi's side of the story, but hold on. I gotta back up a bit before we continue. . . .

Chance

COMPLETELY

freaked out when I told him about the cards Vi had found in Jason's bag.

Who wouldn't? Chance and I planned to skip the craft fair and go straight to the secret gym to figure out our next steps. We knew we needed a solid plan. We agreed to avoid Jason all day and figure out everything after school. Chance told me he was getting out early to feed his neighbor's cat and that he would meet me at the gym. Yeah, looking back, I should have realized it was a red flag.

RED FLAG

What can I say? Guess even geniuses have moments of dumb.

No surprise, Chance never showed up to meet me. And I found this in my locker:

Dash—
So sorry. This is all my fault—my mess, and I'm gonna fix it. I gotta step up and take some action. No more chickening out. I'll see you in the gym in a bit.
Chance

And then things got nuts, all right. I'll let Chance fill you in himself. He's the only one who truly knows what happened.

CHAPTER 9
CHANCE

What's up, Ace?

I'll do my best to describe the events of the day. I was feeling pretty bad at the start of things. I left that note for Dash because there was no other way. Dash and Vi were so cool to me, and all I kept thinking was . . .

this whole mess was all because of me and my stupid mistake.

I mean, if I had ignored those notes in the first place, NONE of this would have happened. And now, with my cards showing up in Jason's backpack? That meant he probably knew about Violet's and Dash's secret identities. I had to worry about him doing something to them, too—not just me.

I felt horrible, and I was really sick and tired of relying on other people for help. It was driving me nuts. First, I chickened out on leaving the note and let Dash down, and

THEN I COMPLETELY FROZE

when Jason bumped into me. I felt so lame. And like Dash always says—we don't wait to be rescued. WE do the rescuing.

I had to do it alone.

So I left the note for Dash and went off to find Jason. When I saw him, I took a deep breath and told myself, Just go up there and do it. Don't be a chicken.

Just go. GO!

Then I heard him ask someone if they had seen Victor.

I thought it was weird.

But it gave me an idea.

I turned the corner, popped into the bathroom, and used my sweet shape-shifting powers.

Good thing we've been spending so much time with Victor at the gym— transforming into him without a picture was a breeze.

I walked back out of the bathroom as Victor and found Jason.

You won't believe what happened.

JASON: Hey, dude. I'm out. Don't ask me for anything else.

ME: Why? What's your problem?

JASON: It's just not worth it. I'm done.

ME: Your loss.

(I knew I had to get outta there before my sixty or so seconds were up. I was about to walk away when Jason reached into his pocket and handed me an envelope.)

JASON: I'm serious. I'm not going to spy on those guys anymore. So take this back. I don't even want it.

(I looked in the envelope and saw money. My brain was working so fast, I didn't know how to react.)

JASON: So we're cool? I thought you'd be mad.

ME: It's cool.

(At this point, I could feel my body vibrating with anger and shock. Plus, any second I was going to shift back to myself!)

Jason: Yeah, find some other sap to carry out your creepy little tasks.

I slipped back into the bathroom just in time.

Thankfully, nobody was there, because they would have had quite a show. I transformed back into myself before even reaching the stall.

I got outta school as fast as I could and hurried to the rec center to find you guys while trying to sort all this junk out in my head.

Why had Victor paid Jason?

What was
going on?

Was

VICTOR
THE
NOTE
WRITER?

I had to find you, Dash, and in that moment,
I really wished I had your Super speed!

Who doesn't?

So I went straight to the gym. Oddly, the front door was locked. I called for you guys and knocked, but nobody answered. I figured you just couldn't hear me. I went around back and saw this ladder leaning against the side of the gym.

I climbed up and opened the window.

And I fell onto a landing.

Then the floor was yanked out from under me and I fell down into a cage. I could barely make out what looked like a tank of water under the cage. Suddenly, the lights came on, and I could see Gigi in a cage on the other side of the gym.

We both were trapped!

CHAPTER 10

VIOLET AND DASH

This was where I came in. When I couldn't find Gigi at the craft fair, I figured I'd check in with Dash and Chance. I guessed they'd be in the gym. By the time I got there, I saw Dash outside, trying to find a way in. He told me the gym was locked and he couldn't find Chance. I told him I hadn't seen Chance or Gigi, and neither of us had seen Victor. So we were both outside wondering what was going on.

Then we heard voices coming from inside the gym—it was Gigi and Chance. I tried the door again, and this time it was

UNLOCKED.

We went inside and were shocked to see our friends locked up in these weird cages on opposite sides of the gym!

Chance yelled,

"It's a trap!"

Then Gigi shouted,

"Get outta here!"

As soon as we started walking toward the cages, Victor appeared. He was standing in the middle of the gym, like the ringmaster of some kind of creepy circus.

Yup. That describes it pretty well. And then Victor was like,

"Welcome, Dash and Violet Parr. This is your final test."

I thought it was some kind of sick joke, but he was totally serious. He kept going, explaining the details of his "final test." He said something like "You will only have enough time to save one of your friends. You have thirty seconds until they are plunged into the water below them. As soon as you release one from their cage, the other one will be dropped into the water." Then he smirked and reached for the timer. But before he hit it, he added,

"So, who will it be? A Normal? Or a Super? The choice is yours. I know who I'd pick."

I thought Victor had lost his mind.

"What are you talking about?"

I shouted.

"How is this a test? What are you even testing us on?"

Victor ignored me and yelled,

"Thirty seconds . . . GO!"

He smacked the timer, and the cages started to lower toward the water tanks!

The following thirty seconds went something like this:

00:00—00:01 seconds: Chance yelled and pointed at Gigi, telling us to save her. (I knew he was still feeling responsible for the whole mess, so he wanted us to save Gigi and not him. That was some true Super thinking, right? I've taught him well.)

00:01—00:08 seconds: Vi said we needed to drain the water from the tanks. If the cages dropped into the water, we wouldn't be able to get Gigi and Chance out in time. Vi jumped on the gym scooter and created a force field around each of her fists. She stuck her arms straight out. I rammed her into the tank beneath Gigi's cage, and her force-field fists cracked the glass!

It was pretty cool. But I think I freaked out Gigi, because I heard her yell, "YOU'RE A SUPER??"

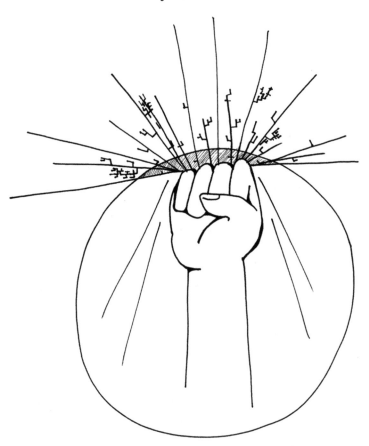

The water started to trickle out of the crack as Victor shook his head and said, "Bad choice. Precious time wasted on a Normal."

00:08—00:15 seconds: Vi and I did our smashing routine on the scooter again—this time crashing into Chance's tank.

Victor laughed. "Nice try, but the weight of the mechanism will crush them if they don't get out of those cages. It's actually worse without the water. You just gave yourself less time. Tick-tock."

Chance yelled,

"Don't listen to anything he says! He's a LIAR! He LIED about Jason!"

Gotta interrupt the time line here—Vi and I were way too focused on the rescue to think about what Chance had said, but I think we were both like, WHAAAAT?! Part of me was, anyway. The other part was noticing the long rope hanging from the ceiling—the rope I had used to practice climbing on. Vi saw me see it, and we looked at each other for a millisecond. One thing that's really cool about having a Super sister like Vi is that we have this connection when we work to fight evil together . . . like we're psycho and we know exactly what the other person is thinking.

*★ * ★★ *★ ★. *

Psychic, Dash. PSYCHIC. Not psycho.

★ ★ ★★ ★★. ★ ★★

In that millisecond, Vi and I knew exactly what we were going to do next.

Okay. Back to the time line:

00:15–00:17 seconds: I jumped onto the rope that was hanging from the ceiling, looped it through the tops of both cages, and dragged it as far as it would go.

00:17–00:23 seconds: I ran as fast as I could (whoo-hoooo!) up the walls and threw the rope over the ceiling pipes! I caught the rope on the other side and ran holding it, causing the cages to rise away from the tanks and toward each other. That's right. I know science. Hello, simple machine. It. Was.

AWESOME!

00:23–00:27 seconds: Vi threw force fields at the locks on the cages until they broke! Go, sis!

00:27–00:30 seconds: Chance and Gigi climbed out of the cages and jumped down to the mats below just as the timer buzzed. I let go of the rope and we all took cover as the cages spun away from each other and crashed to the floor.

We were together in a huddle when Victor floated, all smug, toward the center of the room.

VICTOR: You all fail.

CHANCE: Victor planned everything. HE wrote the notes.

(Before Violet and I could respond, Victor was standing right in front of us.)

VICTOR: Yeah, I wrote the notes. (He walked over to Chance and got right in his face.) And you helped me find more Supers without even delivering on the school records, so thank you for that. (He turned and smiled at me and Violet in this creepy way. Then he floated up, facing us.) Unfortunately, you have all been tested . . . and you have all FAILED. I thought you could be true Supers and join my team. But now I see that you're just as foolish as your parents—putting a Normal's life ahead of a Super's.

VIOLET: You're wrong, Victor.

ME: Being a Super is about protecting people and fighting for GOOD.

CHANCE: It's NOT about DOMINATING! (He sounded angrier than I've ever heard him before.)

VICTOR: You don't think so? What will you do when the rest of us take over the world?

Then he stepped aside and there was another Victor floating in Chance's face.

Then another.
Then another.

In the blink of an eye, Victors were

EVERYWHERE.

Everything happened really fast. The army of Victors started attacking us! And let me tell you,

this was
NOT a guy
who was
new to his
powers.

He could do a lot more than levitate. He could

multiply—
like,
infinitely!

Okay, okay. Vi's reading over my shoulder and keeps bugging me to let her finish the story. She's saying I've gone on too long and it's her turn. Take it away, Vi!

So then all these Victors started coming out of every corner—we couldn't get away from them! We did NOT see that coming.

I stood in front of Gigi, blocking Victor's punches and kicks with flying force fields. It was tough trying to keep up with them all. I think Gigi was still in shock over everything she was seeing.

One Victor stood at the ball machine, shooting tennis balls at us.

Three Victors headed toward Chance. He shape-shifted into a falcon and flew at them, clawing, scratching, and pecking.

Just as another Victor was about to whack Gigi from behind, Dash sprinted over and pushed her out of the way.

I rushed to Gigi to make sure she was all right, but when Dash stopped running, two Victors suddenly descended on him with a net. Three more came out of nowhere to hold the net and make sure Dash couldn't escape.

Gigi was breathless but unhurt.

"I'm okay, Vi. Go help Dash!"

I turned invisible and snuck up behind the Victors. I threw my force-field blades at the net to release Dash. It ripped open, and Dash sped out of there like a rocket before the Victors even noticed the hole. All the Victors screamed in frustration—and turned on me. I threw force-field disks at them as fast as I could, but they dodged and levitated over each one. Then Dash came zooming back—

punching,

kicking, and

tripping

the Victors as he went.

In the meantime, Chance's clock ran out and he turned back into himself. A group of Victors descended on him. Then he shape-shifted again . . . into a cat.

Like, the fluffiest cat I've ever seen.

It was an odd choice, to say the least. Chance could turn into a T. rex and a rhino, but he decided to go with a fluffy kitty?

I have to interrupt here with a little explanation.

FLASHBACK.
Remember when we found out about Victor and the gym?

After I showed him some of my speedy skills and Chance ran through some animals that he could shift into without his cards? I didn't mention it in the journal because it didn't seem important at the time, but when I told Chance to turn into a cat that day, Victor tried to get me to skip it. He was like,

"A cat? That sounds too easy. How about something bigger?"

I insisted because it was Chance's best shift. He was always able to stay in the cat form longer than any other. We clocked him at a whole sixty-five seconds once!

Anyway, we weren't going to skip it—part of the practice is NOT skipping. Chance turned into the cat, and Victor quickly said,

"Let's see another."

He sneezed and reached for some tissues, and he kept up the sneezing for the rest of the afternoon.

Okay.

Back to you, Vi!

I threw a big force field out there, trying to trap as many Victors as I could, when Dash shouted, "Put Chance and me in it, Vi! And try to fit in all the Victors!"

I had no idea what Dash had up his sleeve. Why would he want to be trapped <u>inside</u> the force field with the Victors? But one thing about battling evil together—you have to trust each other. So I released the force field, took a deep breath, and tried again, this time putting Chance the cat and Dash inside, along with what I thought was every single one of the Victors.

It was the

BIGGEST

and most

AWESOME

force field Vi has ever made!

All the Victors inside the force field began to react to Chance the cat. They were sneezing, coughing, and wiping their watering eyes. So yeah, I quickly understood the fluffy-cat plan.

But it turns out I'd missed one Victor. He sprinted toward me, trying to break my focus. Gigi stepped right in front of him, saying, "I got this, Vi!" Then she whispered, "Where's my uncle when you need him, right?"

All I could think was:

I KNEW IT.

Gigi <u>did</u> know about her uncle, Frozone! But there wasn't time to dwell on that. Meanwhile, Gigi started showing off some serious martial arts moves!

The Victor fighting Gigi started feeling the effects of the cat allergy, too—like they were all connected. I stayed focused on the force field, but I was really shocked by some of Gigi's skills. I guess she knew what I was thinking, because she said,

"Six years of judo finally paying off,"

as if answering the question I didn't ask. How cool is she?

So back in the force field, a few of the Victors tried to grab Chance. Dash started zooming around in the bubble. Everything inside began to whip up, creating this crazy Victor-cat-Dash snow globe!

It not only confused and disoriented all the Victors, but one by one, each of them began to wheeze and cough more and more. As the Victors got weaker, they disappeared.

I released the force field, and fluffy-cat Chance pounced on the Victor that Gigi was fighting. The clone sniffled and wheezed until he disappeared, too!

Chance shifted back into his true form. We all looked around for a moment, expecting to see another Victor hiding somewhere, but he was GONE. Every single one of the Victors had VANISHED.

We defeated a super villain with teamwork . . . and a cat. Who knew?

CHAPTER 11
VIOLET
AND
DASH

Jeez. After the ordeal at the gym, we've all been trying to just take one big super-gigantic breath. Gigi and I are all good again. Actually, we're better than before. She dropped this off for me last night. . . .

V—

I'm so sorry. I'm sorry I got angry, and I'm sorry you were forced to keep such a big secret for so long. You're not only a real friend, you're the best. I made this for you—it's something I've been working on. Hope you like it.

♡ G

I wrote her an apology note, too, telling her how much I appreciate her friendship and how I hated hiding that stuff from her. She totally understood. And we both agreed—it was a bad situation, but at least something good came out of it. Now she knows everything, and we can be honest with each other. And it turns out that

Gigi's gift to me.

I love it!

Super Friends G+V

even though Gigi doesn't have Super powers, Supers have seemed normal to her because of her uncle—and she would never reveal his secret. But she'd always wondered whether I knew about Lucius, because our families are so close. I know for an absolute fact that I can trust her with my secret. It feels like I've been holding up a brick wall that I can finally put down. Major relief.

It's a little crazy. I now have a true friend—and I've never had that before. The only other people who know everything about me are my family. Having a real friend is just so . . . cool. I'm working on a necklace for her, too. It's not done yet, but what do you think?

BLECH.

So many feelings.

Reading your mush-fest with Gigi—who, yeah, I know, okay, I'll admit it: she's NOT a villain. Although . . . what if SHE was really pulling the strings with Victor?!

What do you say to THAT theory?!

Seriously, Dash?

Actually, I'm happy that Vi can be all mushy and corny with Gigi now, too. I won't have to read her whining about how she can't talk to her best friend about her powers and blah, blah, blah.

And I'll confess . . .

Chance and I had our corny moment, too.

No, we didn't make each other jewelry, but we did make each other pot holders.

Friends Forever

To My Best Bud

KIDDING!

We had a little— very little—mush-fest of our own.

We apologized to each other and agreed to be honest. I know we did that once before, but this time we

REALLY

mean it.

And I told Chance I got why he wanted to handle Jason on his own. I was impressed, actually—I think that means we have officially boosted his confidence. He was willing to take charge.

That means something, right?

So now we're expecting things to be pretty quiet—at least for a day or so. Oh—Chance did find another note in his locker. We're calling it Victor's Final Farewell.

Here it is:

You are weak. Your powers are wasted on you. Enjoy them while they last, because when the rest of us dominate, you and your friends will regret it.

We all just laughed it off.

Victor's the weak one.

We found out he left town, and we're hoping this note is the last we hear from him. Chance and I still can't believe how cool he seemed at first.

Another lesson learned, I guess.

And hey—
the journal worked.

We caught our perp, didn't we.

I think this is a good way to keep things in check. Who knows what could happen as the battle between good and evil in Municiberg continues?

We shall never slumber!

Although a tiny break might be nice. You know, a wise older sister once told me

I should find a balance.

So . . . what do you think, Vi? How about you, Gigi, Chance, and I go have some normal fun together?

"Normal fun?"

Normal doesn't look so boring anymore, huh? Sounds like a plan. I got us tickets to that movie about the unlikely heroes who try to save the world from giant evil slugs.

WICKED COOL!

Let's watch someone else do the work.

Why are we still writing?

Let's go!

I guess Jack-Jack had to get in on the Parr kid journal, too. I'm going to translate it:

"My big sister and brother are the best!"

Nah. I am trilingual—completely fluent in Spanish, English, and Jack-Jack. That clearly says

"My big brother and sister are the best!"

THE
END